I0649401

Theodora De Wolf Colt

Stray Fancies

Theodora De Wolf Colt

Stray Fancies

ISBN/EAN: 9783337275150

Printed in Europe, USA, Canada, Australia, Japan

Cover: Foto ©Andreas Hilbeck / pixelio.de

More available books at **www.hansebooks.com**

BY

Mrs. THEODORA De WOLF COLT.

BOSTON:
PUBLISHED FOR PRIVATE CIRCULATION.
1872.

TO MY BELOVED SON,

SAMUEL POMEROY COLT,

BY WHOSE EARNEST SOLICITATIONS THE FOLLOWING PIECES WERE

RESCUED FROM THAT OBLIVION WHICH, I FEAR, THAT ALL,

EXCEPT A FEW LENIENT FRIENDS, MAY THINK

THAT THEY DESERVE, THIS VOLUME IS

AFFECTIONATELY DEDICATED

BY THE AUTHOR.

PREFACE.

The verses contained in this volume have been collected and published as they now appear, solely for the relatives and friends of the author.

Some of them bear a personal and local interest, and therefore will be best appreciated by those who are acquainted with the circumstances to which they refer ; while others, it is hoped, may possess some interest for all.

A few of the pieces may perhaps seem to be censorious ; the characters delineated in them are, however, merely the type of a class, and do not refer to individuals.

Many of the poems have appeared in print, in the daily papers, etc., from time to time, but the majority of them have never before been published.

ERRATA.

Page 22 — line 11, 3rd word should be "pallor."

Page 99 — last verse, line 2, "McLellan" should read "McClellan."

Page 100 — verse 2, line 1, 5th word read "a."

Page 126 — line 2, for "darkey" read "donkey."

"T. DeW. Colt" was intended for back of cover, instead of "DeWolf Colt."

Page 122 — line 1, 3rd and 4th words transposed.

CONTENTS.

ON HEARING A GENTLEMAN DECLARE HIMSELF A "SECESSIONIST."

TREADS there a man on Northern soil,
Whose brain is clear and strong,
Who can unblushingly avow
He swells the traitor throng?

"A traitor!" Spoken with contempt
In every clime and age,
And branded with the curse of Cain
On Scripture's sacred page!

I scorn the man who dare disown
Allegiance to his land,—
Who fain would fill the foeman's ranks,
And lend a helping hand.

B   9

I fear in love, the same as war,

    He'd act a dastard's part;

I would not trust him with .my hand,

    My honor, or my heart.

False to his brother and himself,

    His country and his God,

What proof have I that he would keep

    To me his plighted word?

Though at the altar he might swear

    To love me as his bride,

I know some wanton would have power

    To lure him from my side.

Women are brave and loyal too,

    And in their secret souls

They deem each traitor band composed
Of cowards and of fools.

We may not fight, — but we are strong
To show revengeful ire;
And in our bosom brightly burns
Pure patriotic fire.

Thank God! our State's disgraced by few
Who scorn their country's flag,
And raise "Palmetto colors" high
And play "the game of brag."

We've patriots left who offer arms
To fight the Southern foe,
And when *our powder* they demand,
Reply "It is no go!"*

* Alluding to the reply of Col. Hazard, of Enfield, Conn., when asked by the
South to sell them powder, at the commencement of the late Rebellion.

My fervent prayer ascends on high
That God will spare our land —
Avert the doom — unite our foes
In one strong, loving band.

But if 'tis otherwise ordained,
And war's relentless might
Must desolate her fields and spread
Its universal blight,

O may New England's sons stand firm
As ancient chivalry,
And bravely fight for home and right,
Truth, God and Liberty!

EMANCIPATION.

A PALL o'erspread our land,
And all were blanched with fear, —
The mighty incubus oppressed
The people far and near.

Some feared the helm of state
Was not directed sure, —
That 'twixt the whirlpool and the rock
No ship could long endure.

But a mighty man stood there, —
Strong, honest, brave, and true ;

With firm right arm he steered the craft,

And crashing she went through :

Through, spite of traitor tongue, —

Despite of traitor foe, —

He crushed their malice, doffed their might,

By one determined blow.

At the foul fiend he struck

They in their breasts kept warm,

Who, adder-like, stung them to death

When guarded from the storm.

One hour perchance of doubt,

One prayer to God for aid, —

Then a bold stroke of daring pen

Three million freemen made.

Free from the torturing lash,

From brutal lust and power,

From the wild shriek of wife and child,

Parted in bitter hour.

Free to become true men,

To own the soil they till,

To know themselves, and learn the place

They may with justice fill.

The God of armies then

Fought with us for the true,

And soon our Flag on every height,

Replaced the "Traitor Blue."

A ·LADY sat in her tower lone,

Nursing a thought she might not own;

She leans her cheek on her white hand,

Heeds not the music of her band.

Sudden a woman's wail of woe

Fell on her ear, acute but low;

She rose, and ere she reached the door,

One sank beside her on the floor:

"O lady! a tale I have to tell

Of the direst grief that e'er befell, —

My lord struck in the chase to-day,

As if by chance, Sir Malcolm Grey.

My husband saw the dreadful deed,—

Unstanched the wound was left to bleed;

But were it known that he took note

Not worth his life a single groat."

The lady stood as turned to stone,—

Sight, hearing, touch, alike were flown,

For in our hour of deepest grief

The soul disdains such poor relief,

As 'outward vent of sigh or tear,—

The fount's afar, the woe is here,

Crushing and deadly in its might,

Each sense benumbed with sudden fright,

To all emotion seeming dead,

The blood a frozen stream of lead:

So to endure, some have been known,

The surgeon's knife without a groan.

A tap was heard at the door, so light,

And entered there a youthful knight,

His hunter's suit of forest green

Became his high and haughty mien;

His broidered sash was loosely tied,

A silver pouch hung by his side,

A pluméd cap drooped o'er his brow,

But doffed before the lady now;

Upon his bold, bad, handsome face,

Each passion vile had left a trace;

His eyes, once soft, cerulean blue,

A baneful light now glittered through

Those loopholes of the soul where sin

Lets the angel out and devil in;

Graceful and brave, but false and foul,

Such was "the lord of Stony Owl."

"Sweet one, methinks thy cheek is pale,

While mine is ruddy from the gale ;

Your hand is cold as any stone,

But I will warm it in my own."

He kissed her lips, and then he placed

His murderous arm around her waist,

But she shrinks not from his caress,

Hears not his words of tenderness:

"Dearest, I have a fete prepared,

Assembled are each knight and laird :

. The rubies you must wear to-night,

They best become your beauty bright.

That serpent with the quaint device,

An heir-loom ours for centuries twice ;

His head a flaming ball of fire,

With diamond eyes to pierce desire ;

His tongue a thread of silver steel

To smoothly cut and keenly feel.

(Of him a curious legend told:

How that a knight and lady bold,·

Fleeing in darkness and in sin

To hide her shame from all within,

Were by him sorely stung to death,

Their bones left whitening on the heath.)

When coiled within thy glossy hair

What lover brave his suit will dare?

Put on the cross of liquid red,

(It gives the wearer pain 'tis said,)

Then add the brilliant blazing zone,

And I will know thee all my own."

Still like a statue there she stands,

No blood within those marble hands;

The maidens proudly deck her form,

The fiery rubies fail to warm :

Her beauty so unlike to earth,

In other sphere perchance had birth,

As if the burning hue of Mars,

With the pale light of softer stars,

Combined to form a perfect whole :

Thus on our sight the vision stole.

He led her to a darkened room,

With stifled dampness like a tomb,

Only a single ray of light

Dispelled the blackness of the night ;

It fell upon a velvet pall

Which hung suspended from the wall,

But turned aside might soon disclose

A waxen form in death's repose.

She sees, she feels, she knows all now, —

C

Leaps the hot blood from cheek to brow;

Wildly she rushes to the spot

Where Malcolm is and yet is not;

Falls on the fearful coffin lid

So heavily, that from it slid

The crackling glass, its cutting pain

Crazing still more her heart and brain.

She drags·him fiercely to her breast,

The warm blood stains his snowy vest,

Dyes the bright rubies richer red,

Changes the palor of the dead;

With shrieks that pierced each corridor

She then sank senseless on the floor.

Her lord has ta'en another bride,

But never sleeps he by her side;

With many in the chase takes part,

Never to one unfolds his heart ;

Says that " There is no room in life

But for one friend and for one wife,"

Tho' the friend lies beneath the sward,

And the wife under watch and ward.

"WAITING FOR THE MORROW."

WOULD you like to hear my story?
  Then please sit in the corner there,
And I'll tell it while arranging
  In bright clustering curls, my hair.

You must know I'm to be married
  Whene'er the morrow shall come,
And I watch eagerly for it
  As I pace up and down the room.

My lover he left me this morning,
  With a spirit gay as a bird —

And his laugh I hear resounding

When I repeat his parting word.

And he said, "My darling, to-morrow

These pearls will your white neck entwine,

But far more priceless the jewel

I have found to encircle mine."

But now comes an hour of blackness,

Of terror and frenzied despair ;

My heart seemed a great ball of fire,

And demons were tearing my hair.

Some tale they told me I wot not,

Of a boat upset in the stream,

A corpse all tangled in seaweed —

But I know 'twas only a dream.

*C

See, this is the hair they brought me,

   With which I have played all the day,

And placed it oft on my forehead,

   And as oft it was blown away.

Here I sit waiting the morrow,

   And so sadly my thoughts do roam,

For I am weary of waiting

   And longing to go to my home.

It is a cottage so lovely,

   A cottage away by the sea,

New, refined, fragrant, and cozy,

   Just fitted for true love and me.

It was yesterday we went there,

   And he showed me a pretty room,

Filled with pictures, books and statues

    And rare flowers of rich perfume.

Then he flung his strong arms round me

    And drew me close to his broad breast,

And a thrill of joy comes o'er me

    When I think of that place of rest.

And sometimes when I am sleeping

    He seems o'er my bed to stand,

And says, "My darling, I'm waiting

    For thee in a far better land.

But I know it is a vision,

    For so speedily it is flown;

And he would never leave me thus

    So desolate, weary and lone.

Oft when I awaken I say

"O surely to-morrow is here,"

Then I put on my white satin

And my other rich bridal gear.

But the dress seems quite old-fashioned,

And the shoes are all soiled and torn,

The buds from the orange-wreath fallen,

Although it has never been worn.

Then one will come to me laughing,

And whisper, "Why are you so gay?"

And if I ask "Is it to-morrow?"

Will reply "Oh no, it's to-day."

My neck is wrinkled and yellow,

My dark hair begins to look white,

My eyes have grown dim with weeping

And watching this wearisome night.

I polish the gems in cases —

I gaze at the ring on my hand —

I fold and refold my dresses,

And wind the small watch on my stand.

"Oh, can it be that the morrow

Came and went in the drear blank time,

That my love grieved not to find me

And so passed to another clime?

I know not — and now am sleepy,

But please wake me in time to dine,

To-morrow we're to wed early

And breakfast is ordered at nine."

THE PARTING OF SIBYL AND HASTINGS.

WITHIN a costly chamber sat
    A maid of courtly fame,
For beauty not for birth renowned,
    And Sibyl is her name.

Her dark eye has a wistful gaze,
    A flush is on her cheek,
A finger on her rosy mouth,
    As if she feared to speak.

She listens; ah, she hears a sound,
    And sure some one is there:

'Tis he! the loved one has returned,
　His step is on the stair.

One bound, and she is in his arms,
　·Her head is on his breast,
For all her grief is well repaid,
　At last has found her rest.

The wondrous thrill of ecstacy,
　The transport and the bliss, —
What poet's pen has power to paint,
　Of such an hour as this?

The human heart for once has all
　Of rapture it can hold,
Ages of lesser happiness
　Are in that moment told.

Were heaven opened to our view

By some magician's spell,

Celestial joys I fear we'd spurn,

And love the earth too well.

But quick as thought the maiden turned,

That dream of joy had past;

She turned and of the haughty lord,

This question mildly asked:

"Hast thou in exile found a bride,

More loved than Sibyl, speak?"

He speaks not, falters, 'tis too true,

Be still, my heart, or break.

"Sibyl," began the conscious lord,

"O answer me, pray do!"

"Well, be it so, my task is done;

What thou hast said is true."

She did not weep, she did not faint,

And from her lips no cry;

Naught but her marble cheek disclosed

Her fearful agony.

And then by effort strong and vast,

Which exhausts years of life,

She said unto her faithless lord:

"Depart, and seek thy wife.

Farewell, Lord Hastings, nothing more

Is needed now; depart,

And Heaven bless both thee and thine,—

I pray this from my heart."

D

"No, Sibyl, you must hear my tale:—
I sought you once in vain
To place you in my heart of hearts
Had Fate so wove the chain.

You know how well I loved in youth,
A high-born, handsome dame,
And that her kinsman parted us
'Till I could win a name.

She wed another, and in wrath
I spurned her from my soul;
But on his death soon learned from her
The act was by control.

She followed me in exile drear,
To a far distant land,

Then out of gratitude and love
 I offered her my hand.

I knew not when the war would cease,
 Or if we then should meet :—
I dare not say I love thee still ;
 Forgive me, I entreat."

"I do forgive thee," Sibyl cried,
 "And pray that Heaven may shed
Its choicest gifts on thee and her
 Whom thou hast lately wed.

O may she love thee tenderly,
 And cherish thee as well,
As fondly, as I would have done,"
 And now the tear-drops fell.

"Thank God," said Hastings, "that my fault
   At least has left thee pure;
Another love may warm thy heart
   ' And all thy sorrows cure."

Now the wronged Sibyl showed her pride,
   And turned her flashing eye
As a bold wounded eagle might
   Upon the sportsman nigh:

"Many a lesson, noble lord,
   Perchance I learned of thee,
But there is one you fail to teach —
   . That love can transferred be.

"Think you I'd give my wasted heart
   And take one in return?

That Passion has not yet worn out
  Where love may brightly burn?

O coarse and rude belief of man,
  If the mere form be pure,
There's nothing lost that truth and peace
  And wedded bliss insure.

Where is the bloom of sinless thought
  Ne'er found on earth again? .
Gone with the treasure of thy love,—
  Go seek it then in vain.

Shall I to lover pledge my troth
  And fealty swear, while now
Upon my lips doth burn the kiss
  With which we sealed our vow?
*D

449816

You never felt the maddening spell
    That chains my spirit fast;
You cannot dream the depth of love
    That must forever last."

Then with an agonizing sob .
    Into his arms she fell,
And with one passionate caress
    He took a last farewell.

O Hastings! falsehood never yet
    Sullied thy lips to man;
Why break thy faith with woman then?
    Pray answer, if you can.

And in thy evil hour of doom,
    Of stars and splendor shorn,

Mayst think the falcon's beak was sharp

With which he kissed that morn.*

Sweet Sibyl, learn that love like thine,

So free from earthly leaven,

Finds no congenial soil below,—

It only blooms in Heaven.

* Alluding to the words of the tymbesteres.

THE LAMENT.

I'M seated on the rock, Annie—
The one so near the shore;
But lonely are the waves, Annie,—
I sigh for thee once more.

I miss thy hand in mine, Annie,
Thy gentle tones of love,
With the summer breeze to fan us,
And the bright stars above.

Dost remember one night, Annie,
When the moon shone on high,

And softly fell its rays, Annie,

And kissed both you and I?

But do not mistake me, Annie,

It was the moon I said,

But will confess she tempted me

To take her place instead.

But now I'm all alone, Annie,

And can do naught but weep

For the sweet words and earnest vows

I trust that you will keep.

Then do not forget me, Annie,

This cold November night,

For love is like the sun, Annie,

To keep us warm and bright.

And let no other love, Annie,

    Find place within thy heart,

But be true as steel, my Annie,

    Then God alone can part.

SLIGHTED GIFTS.

I GAVE thee once a lovely flower
  Thy home to render bright,
For thee to guard with jealous eye
  And nurture day and night.

I gave to thee a perfume rare,
  Too seldom found on earth,
But from the swects of Paradise
  Selected for its worth.

Another sacred gift was thine,
  A pure and peerless gem,

43

Whose spotless lustre well adorned

A seraph's diadem.

Where is the flower?—its petals drooped

Without thy watchful care;

'Twas worn upon a stranger's breast;

Alas! it withered there.

The perfume so despised by thee

Another dared inhale,

But to inspire his grosser sense

Fragrance from Heaven must fail.

The gem unprized, neglected, scorned,

One sought to make his own,

But soon 'neath his unhallowed touch

He mourned its lustre gone.

The casket that these gifts enshrined,

Though worthless deemed by thee,

Was not denied a place within

The realms of Deity.

Dost marvel when these treasures rare

Were ever owned in life?

I gave them all when I bestowed

Thy young and gentle wife.

Beauty, and love, and innocence,

The flower, perfume, and gem,

But valueless alike to thee

Until deprived of them.

By coldness, perfidy, and scorn

Each did in turn depart,

E

And left behind a fearful wreck,
A blighted human heart.

The wily tempter promised all
Thy right alone to give,
To every wound applied a balm,
And bade the victim live.

But tho' in dark and sinful paths
Awhile she dared to roam,
Jesus with earnest love reclaimed
And brought the wanderer home.

A life of penitence and woe
For His dear sake was blest,
And angels wiped her tears away
And welcomed her to rest.

The contrite sinner's humble prayer

  Is ne'er despised by me ;

For such as these the Saviour died,

  But not for such as thee.

Tho' heaped with honors upon earth,

  Before me thou dost stand

In thy own utter worthlessness,

  ·Among the outcast band.

Beside thee he who falsely· lured

  A chosen one of mine,

His sin must meet its punishment, —

  A greater one is thine.

For thou didst glory in thy shame,

  And deem thyself misused,

Nor ever breathed one fervent prayer
  For all my gifts abused.

Now for thy unrepentant soul
  This shall the torture be :
Eternal consciousness of self —
  Eternal loss of me.

FALL OF THE LINDENS.

SEPTEMBER 8, 1869.

ALL nature seemed lulled in a calm repose,

Not a breath disturbed the leaves of the rose;

Windows were raised to let in the cool air,

But a stifling vapor, all that was there.

Before a broad mansion some lindens stood,

They had named themselves "The pride of the wood."

Rugged and tall, as formed for each gale,

Not even Envy could hint they were frail.

*E   49

A lady observes them with marked delight,

'Till she hears a loved voice, cheerful and bright;

And one then advances close to her side

On whom she looks with affection and pride:

It is a beaming face, unstained by sin,

Undisturbed by passion raging within,

Unsullied and calm as a silvery lake

On which angry billows ne'er toss and break;

And yet not deficient in strength of mind,

But formed "to combat with his kind."

He gazed awhile on the grand old trees,

And said: "I'd not take a fortune for these."

The proud lindens thought, "We'll treasure that word,

And a sweeter sound we have never heard,

For even if wood should chance to be dear

We'll not be cut down from our places here:

And where is the wind that will be so bold

To topple us down from our standing old?

Now the sweet orange-tree deems itself rare,

In a hot-house raised with such tender care,

But it cannot endure the cold and gale,

Soon nipped by the frost or killed by the hail,

While we set at defiance age and clime,

And raise our tall heads in spite of old Time."

The storm-king abroad heard their boasting vain,

And said: " Those proud Lindens are *at it again ;*

I've tried them oft with my strength and power,

But well they have flourished until this hour;

But one other effort I will make soon

To bring down their tall pride this afternoon."

With that he rustled his terrible wings,

And the motion shook terrestrial things;

Church steeples trembled, high chimneys came down,
And the racket was great throughout the town;
Large trees were uplifted, small boats unmoored,
And many a sign-board quickly floored;
But each linden laughed in frolicsome glee, —
" I defy the storm-king to injure me."

But there comes a sad day, alas! to all,
When the pride we have nursed must have a fall;
And the stalwart trees felt the powerful breath
Of one who could deal them the stroke of death.
But they fought him well, in their branches tied
They hugged him so tight he liked to have died,
And they did not yield one inch of the ground
Without a fierce struggle for their roots sound,
And we doubted whether it might not be
That at last they would win the victory.

They knew that the dreaded old monster's might

Ceased often upon the approach of night,

And longed as much as "the Duke" for that hour

When most he felt Napoleon's power.

But now the stern contest began to tell

On the foremost one in the rank, who fell

So heavily on the one by his side

That he in turn leaned on his comrade tried,

And when once that serried force gave way,

The storm-king victorious won the day.

The mocking sun rose the ensuing morn

On a place all desolate and forlorn ;

The old lindens grand, in their might laid low,

Nor spared to us even an apple-blow.

But gracefully stood the orange-tree there,

Not a bud despoiled or a branch laid bare.

THE BLISSFUL HOUR.

THEY may talk of the blissful general

Whose victory now has been won,

Or the bliss of the author whose volume

Has just had a successful run.

Of the lover who has long been sighing,

And obtained his very first kiss,—

But not one of them has the least notion

Of the highest acme of bliss.

May be you think 'tis hearing Parepa

Or some other nightingale squall,

Or driving by the side of your lover

On a moonlight night to a ball.

You have not hit it yet, I can tell you,

But be patient and you shall learn,

And I know full well when you have heard me

That all other bliss you will spurn.

You have been asked, of course, to a party, —

Well, so far, the thing is all right,

But did ever the "modiste" insert you

In a dress two inches too tight?

Did they screw up your hair from the forehead,

And then stick it with pins so fine,

That your whole head appeared to resemble

Most an inverted porcupine.

Were your feet tightly cased in "number two?"
　　Your hands squeezed into "number six?"
The mirror, to tease, a reflection cast
　　That your colors choice failed to mix?

Did you learn from your kindly hostess soon
　　That the one you hoped to have met,
And the only one you cared to see,
　　Had that moment sent a regret?

As you grieved, did the bore, Mr. S—, come near,
　　And glueing himself to your side
Relate that old tale without the least point,
　　If we except the hero died?

And did you think, O, if he were that man,
　　What a world's relief it would be;

And shake him off to find yourself caught
By that odious friend, Miss G. ?

Who simpers with hate, and abuses all
Who may chance to be bright and fair ;
" What a fright's Miss T., just look at the way
That Laura Jones frizzes her hair."

If this were all, but the scandal she serves
Is such an unsavory dish,
I am sometimes tempted to tell her plain,
That it is worse than " ancient " fish.

In the supper-room were you ever crushed,
And have a deluge of ice cream
On the skirt of your pet light satin poured,
And your smile like a martyr's seem ?

F

Then did a sad partner fall to your lot
　　Who was so determined to go
That he set at defiance Time and Tune
　　And constantly trod on your toe?

If so, the bliss you can well understand,
　　Which now I'm about to explain,
And say all other when with it compared,
　　Is low, profitless, weak, and vain.

It is to be safely shut in your room,
　　Where never a soul dare intrude,
To pull down your hair, remove your fine clothes,
　　And the pressure of steel and wood.

A wrapper to don, and tight shoes to doff,
　　That you may place your elastic feet

In slippers it may be of number four,

. But comfortable, warm, and neat.

Then to seat yourself in a large arm-chair,

By a fire so cozy and bright,

And a bliss more sensuous than I can paint

Fills your soul with a strange delight.

More entrancing by far than De Quincey

E'er knew in his opium dream,

A delicious languor enfolds you,

Every thought in Lethe's stream.

No keen feeling of dissatisfaction,

That he, she, or it, is not there;

No dread of a rival outshining you

In a new set of jewels rare.

Not even a wish that you were richer,

Or somebody else was not poor,

But a happiness calm such as never

In any state long can endure.

Such a perfect sense of deliverance

From mental and physical pain,

Without e'en a mosquito to bore you,

Is worth fighting a world to gain.

And now every hero I challenge,

Whether of glory, love, or fame,

To assert in their most triumphant hour

That they have felt the bliss I name.

VINCIT QUI PATITUR.*

[HE CONQUERS WHO ENDURES.]

PRESS boldly onward in the race,

He conquers who endures;

Foremost in battle set thy face.

He conquers who endures.

Be not cast down by trials long,

He conquers who endures;

The prize is given to the strong,

He conquers who endures.

* The De Wolf Motto.

Strive to win riches, fame, and love,

He. conquers who endures ;

But strive far more for joys above,

He conquers who endures.

Let no stain on your honor light,

He conquers who endures,

And keep your Christian armor bright,

He conquers who endures.

Fight Satan with your weapons keen,

He conquers who endures ;

On none but Christ the Saviour lean,

He conquers who endures.

Boldly defend the cause of right,

He conquers who endures,

Make others stronger by thy might,

He conquers who endures.

Fear not to give for truth thy life,

He conquers who endures,

A crown for him who wins the strife,

He conquers who endures.

THE TRUE STORY OF LITTLE RED
RIDING HOOD.

WITHIN a rural village dwelt
  A maiden fair and good,
Named by her friends in sportive jest,
  Their sweet "Red Riding Hood."

A crimson cloak she often wore,
  And crimson bonnet too,
With cheek and lip that far outvied
  Them both in brilliant hue.

All loved her for her pretty ways,
  Freedom from sin and guile,

Felt any favor well repaid,

If they might see her smile.

A maiden's purity, we're told,

Once tamed a savage beast,

But one who saw our little maid,

On her desired to feast.

He was a wolf but well disguised

In clothing of a lamb,

His cloak of soft, warm, glossy wool,

One could not deem a sham.

Often, Red Riding Hood he met,

Returning from a walk ;

Would hide her in his silky cloak,

And have a nice long talk.

His eyes so large and full of fire,
   The gentle girl would fright,
Then he would tell her they were made
   To see her beauty bright.

His nostrils wide were to inhale
   The sweetness of her breath,
His arms to clasp her fairy form,
   And wear her until death. .

The sole wish of his ear to drink
   The music of her voice,
To hear those gentle winning tones
   That made his heart rejoice.

The only purpose of his mouth
   To bite her cherry lip,

To cull its sweetness as the bees
  Honey from roses sip.

And thus he won her maiden heart,
  Without a dream of ill,
The soft warm cloak wherein she lay
  Disguised the monster still.

One day he met her in a wood,
  And said in blandest tone :
" My dearest one, why are you here,
  Disconsolate and lone ? "

She raised to his her blushing face,
  And said, "'Tis hard you see,
But grandma's sick and there are none
  To wait on her but me.

She lives there, just below the hill,
 In a hut worn and old,
It's very poor and hardly serves
 To keep out rain and cold.

"O," said the wolf, "then I will go
 And comfort the old dame,
And take a bag of silver too,
 Though she knows not my name.

And now a little sport we'll have :
 Let me go first, then you,
And the old lady 'll laugh to find,
 I'm not her grand child true.

So poor Red Riding Hood delayed,
 And wandered through the wood,

Plucking each rose without a thought,

Except what boded good.

Until she reached her grandma's door,

Now must my story end,

Her fate perchance the same as all.

Who on a wolf depend.

None who explored that hut e'er told

What shocking sight they saw,

But they inferred the victims both,

Glutted the monster's maw.

For never more in cottage bower

Was Riding Hood e'er seen,

And on May Day no maidens danced

Upon the village green.

G

But there will come a time when *wolves*

Before their Judge must stand;

The blood of all "Red Riding Hoods"

Required at their hand.

CHARITY.

"KIND lady, my mother is sick and poor,

And we cannot keep the wolf from our door,

Ere to-morrow night our rent will be due,

And the landlord stern swears then he will sue,

And take the little we now call our own,

Leaving us homeless, hungry, and alone."

Thus spake a young girl, one bitter cold day,

To a lady walking along Broadway :

A lady so dainty, so nice and fair,

You surely must deem the angel was there ;

One who from youth had served Duty and God,

Whose feet never strayed from the narrow road,

71

Whom all men esteemed, praised, honored, and blest,

Beloved by parents, by sisters caressed.

She carried a well-filled purse in her hand,

And paused, as if fully to understand

The shivering maiden's sad tale of woe,

Ere on Duty's path she hastened to go.

" You must not presume that all in the street

Will give to each beggar they chance to meet.

You may be one who from virtue has swerved,

And faith no longer be placed in your word.

There are places provided for such as you,

I must give to poor friendless ' Timbuctoo ; '

For I have no proof of the tale you tell."

And as honey-dew sweet her accents fell

On her listener's ear, but in her heart

They deeper pierced than a poisoned dart.

A blush of shame crimsoned her honest check

As with quivering voice she strove to speak.

But unfinished the words died in the air,

Only to Heaven arose one wild prayer:

That she and her mother might both be dead

Ere the morning sun should shine on their bed.

A woman who stood quite near to her side,

Had witnessed the scene, and now (as she cried,

Those great tears which well might turn us to stone,

Were we suffered oft to weep them alone,)

Spoke never a word but threw in her lap

A purse so heavy it burst with a snap,

Scattering round her the glittering gold

Like the showers on "Danæ," famed of old;

"Who are you? An angel,—from Heaven you came!

Stop for a moment and tell me your name;

*G

Let me bless you, for well I know that you

Must be all which is noble, just, and true."

"See you yon broad mansion of splendid shame?

Go there if you really would learn my name;

There where the gay and the profligate meet,

And the good shake off the dust from their feet;

Where the wine in goblets of gold is poured,

And the oath with the ribald song is heard,

Where Satan seems loose, so strong is his sway,

And the Decalogue's trampled on each day.

There, from the burning, lascivious lip,

You will hear my name as the wine they sip,

Spoken by all with a jest or a sneer

And never by one with respect or fear;

Baptised from the stagnant fountain of guilt,

Abandoned by God, learn more if thou wilt.

But if to each man belongs my vile name,

My money is ever my own the same;

Though the wages of sin, it is as good

To purchase your mother clothes, fire, and food,

For none will care, when they see its bright sheen,

Whether the donor was soiled or clean.

I have no false hope that the One above

Will look on the deed with approving love.

Full well I know that it cannot atone

For the least foul sin my life may have known;

And I never dare mock His throne with prayer

In my deadliest hour of dark despair;

But having myself been hungry and cold

I pitied your mother, — my tale is told."

She left, and so soon was lost in the crowd

She missed the girl's blessing, sincere not loud,

Who instantly rose and ran to her home,

For fear the rapacious landlord might come.

As soon as she set her foot on the stair,

Spoke that her mother might know she was there,

Then placed on the stand the gold pieces bright

As she entered the room with a heart so light.

"Why, Mary, my child, how came you by these?"

"Honestly, mother." Then down or her knees

The widow sank, humbly praying to God,

That the one who sent to her poor abode

Means for their comfort, might ever be blest

With health, riches, and friends, love, joy, and rest.

And who shall say that the lone widow's prayer,

Thus wafted to Heaven, was not God's care?

That His Spirit may not come, like a dove,

On *her* in the arms of unhallowed love,

And lead her worn, weary, passion-stained soul

To Calvary's cross and there make her whole?

Or that the sad "recording angel's" tear

Shall not fall on her page and wash it clear?

Perchance the angel of Mercy looked down

On "slumbering innocence" with a frown, —

On her whose life to Duty was given,

Who thought it the only road to heaven,

Who ne'er a generous impulse had known,

But who really lived for herself alone;

Who fasted in Lent, and at Easter gave,

And thought by so doing her soul to save.

All this is well, but there is something more

Required ere we can reach Heaven's door.

God gave us our hearts to beat and to feel,

And sympathy sweet that must not congeal,

We have no right to pass the wretched by,

And at last He will know the reason why,

" Ye have passed me by, nor unclosed your hand,

Ye have not relieved the poor in your land.

No orphan's heart have you ever made light,

No lone captive cheered with your presence bright.

Worthy or not, all the slight was to me,

Depart, ye accursed, I never knew ye."

Give when you may, without letting " I could "

Always wait for the heartless, grim " I should."

LIZZIE.

BRIGHT as a brilliant sunbeam,
  Beautiful as a pearl,
A crystal drop from fountain pure,
  Is my pet little girl.

Her every tone is music,
  And falls upon my ear,
Sweet as the song by seraphs sung,
  The throne of God to cheer.

Her dark eyes are so lovely,
  Her every movement grace,

So strangely winning are her ways,
And heaven in her face.

And then she is as happy
As any forest bird,
Chatting and playing merrily,
Never a naughty word.

O may God spare my darling,
My jewel, flower, and sun,
To fill my soul with light until
My days on earth are done.

TO E——. B——.

" O FOR a world where things might be
What now·they only seem,"
Where Claude should be the waking hour,
All else be but a dream.

And Richelieu's curse, by thee pronounced,
The guilty courtier's awe ;
His knowledge force the feeble king
To make his will the law.

Where Hamlet, cruel to be kind,
Should probe his mother's heart,

H 81

Tearing her secret from its folds,
   And wrenching it apart.

Where Macbeth, by the sisters glozed,
   Should rush upon his doom;
Find Macduff not of woman born,
   That Birnam wood had come.

And hump-backed Richard, with sweet words,
   Win the fair Annie's heart,
Showing the weird, strange, dazzling might
   Of intellect and art.

Where the reality should prove
   Young Juliet's dream of bliss,
To lie in Romeo's arms, and feel
   Upon her lips his kiss.

And Benedick, Beatrice win,

  Iago's demon spite

Recoil in vengeance on himself,

  And then "put out the light."

Where old Sir Giles in pain should writhe,

  Who could a daughter's shame

Counsel, if so she were to win

  A coronet and name.

And the poor Stranger, weary, worn,

  Heart-sick of all in life,

Should find, then pity and forgive,

  His loving, erring wife.

Where the brave Brutus should avenge

  The chaste Lucretia's death ;

Reckless Don Cæsar find a wife,
 Life, fortune, in a breath.

Where guilty Mortimer should quake
 Before his servant true ;
Shylock demand his pound of flesh ;
 Petruchio tame the shrew.

If, as philosophers assert,
 Nothing exists but *you*,*
The real world may be the false,
 The mimic one the true.

And who shall say that no deep truths
 Are taught upon the stage ?
That a great actor bears no part
 In a reforming age ?

    * Meaning one's self.

Is there no sermon in the fate

  Of vengeance, lust, and greed,

When they who thus despise God's law,

  Are left in sorest need?

All characters portrayed by thee

  Do really live again,

Not merely puppets pulled by wires,

  But individual men.

Each word of thine is finely cut,

  And polished as a gem ;

Each gesture suited to the word,

  Each action so like them.

Were Claude to paint my bridal home

  With such a voice and eye,
  *H

Then ask me to select an orb,
In which to dwell on high,

I fear, alas, that I might choose
One bright especial star,
Shining so near me in the crowd,
So near, and yet so far.

'Tis said the magic power you wield,
Is fatal to the soul,
A syren song to lure us on
Beyond our self-control.

But if it be dangerous to speak,
And look, and act like you,
One wish comes stealing o'er my soul,—
Would I were dangerous too.

TO ———.

I 'VE sat up late many a night,
　At balls and parties gay;
Have danced sometimes till broad daylight,
　To while the hours away,

At theatre and concert too,
　I've flirted with the beaux;
Have wept when sad, and laughed when gay,
　And loved perchance,—who knows?

And oft a book has chained me fast
　Till witching hour of night,

Or charming converse of a friend
　　Has kept my spirits bright.

But would you learn my darling sport,
　　Prized more than fame or glory,
It is when seated by thy side,
　　We're writing glib our story.

The world to us is nothing then,
　　Comets might rise and set,
Kings be dethroned, and empires won,
　　Calmly we'd write on yet.

One glance from those cerulean eyes,
　　One smile upon that lip,
And the Pierian fount is reached,—
　　Most sweetly can I sip.

For mind on mind hath woundrous power,
  And soul awakens soul,
More rapturous and inspiring far
  Than song or flowing bowl.

Well might the courtier reply,
  When questioned by his king,
As to what magic arts were used
  To win his heart from him.

"Forgive my boldness, gracious liege,
  I am bewitched, I own,
By the same beauty, wit, and grace,
  Which has o'erturned a throne."

Witches of old were gaunt and grey,—
  What fools our grandsires were;

If they had burned the beautiful,

They had been wiser far.

The serpent knew our weakness when

He came in lovely guise;

Age never could have tempted Eve,

She still had closed her eyes.

There is a key unlocks each heart,

And almost owns its spell:

A dangerous gift perchance to those

Who fail to use it well.

But placed within thy careful hand,

None need to fear its power,

Only a subtle influence felt

To charm each passing hour.

And like a sunbeam o'er my soul

   Thy presence brightly steals,

Waking each sense, and every thought

   To thy quick mind reveals.

And when our story's at an end,

   O, may we often meet,

As two congenial spirits may,

   To hold rare converse sweet.

And never may war's dread alarm

   Summon thee from my side ;

Urge thee to leave thy pleasant home,

   And stem its fiery tide.

Thy absence I should mourn in truth,—

   Do not thy life expose ;

Let others go who'll not be missed,
　　To fight their country's foes.

Good folks are scarce, and bright ones too,
　　So stay I do entreat;
Be like Gamaliel me to teach,
　　While seated at thy feet.

You must not leave,— it cannot be,—
　　For I should die of grief;
So change your mind, and with us stay,
　　And give my soul relief.

And many a pleasant plot we'll plan,
　　And many a hero too,
'Till fame shall write our noble names,
　　With th' immortal few.

TO ——, WITH A SUGAR BOWL.

GOLD to the rich, and sweets to those
Who 'neath the honeymoon repose;
" To him that hath more shall be given,"
Such is the blessed word of heaven.

And in Life's bark it must be sweet,
Where beauty, youth, and virtue meet,
To sail beneath the summer sun,
Love, captain, pilot, mate in one.

May adverse gales then ne'er arise
To dim the brightness of the skies,

Nor shoals or quicksands e'er appear,

To warn thee from the harbor near.

May Life's vast sugar bowl o'erflow

With every sweet that mortals know;

And may the gods vouchsafe to lend

Nectar, ambrosia, to their friend.

And should you ever turn to sip

The honey-dew from favored lip,

May no sting teach you that there grows

A thorn beside the fairest rose.

And when you've reached the blessed shore

Of Hymen's banks, to roam no more,

And like the wreath-crowned queen of May,

Life seems but one long holiday,

Then think upon thy absent friend,

Who a slight token fain would send,

Who, as the sparkling glasses meet,

Gives for her toast, "Sweets to the sweet."

TO H. H. B ———.

THE world's gettin' so wise now
  We cant b'lieve nothin' at all;
They've clean wiped out creation,
  The Serpent, Garden, and Fall.

They tell us that the Deluge
  Was but a busted lake,
It wet the airth a little,
  But no great fuss did make.

The Sphynx never had no riddle,
  The Pyramids are a sham,

There wan't no Tower of Babel,

  And never a man called Ham.

They doubt if the whale swallowed Jonah,

  Or if Jonah swallowed the whale;

And say there wan't no Moses

  For Is'rel to bewail.

That Joan of Arc was a fizzle,

  John Rogers did'nt roast,

And St. Lawrence on the gridiron

  Never made a famous toast.

That Tell did'nt shoot the apple,

  George Washington would lie,

And Methusaleh was no older

  Than either you or I.
  *I

They doubt if Bluebeard ever

    Killed all his seven wives;

If the Sun moves around us,

    Or if cats have nine lives.

They say David wan't no model,

    King Arthur was a myth;

There wan't no " Pokyhontas,"

    Only A-dam Smith.

That Columbus didn't discover

    The land he didn't name;

That th' Egyptians knowed on't,

    And ancients all the same.

That the Catacombs were never

    Receptacles for the dead;

That Michael Angelo did n't paint

"The Last Judgment" on his head.

That Raphael's Madonna

Was a lady of ill fame,

And that it was n't Grouchy

Spoiled Napoleon's little game.

That Richelieu was no statesman,

And Crœsus was 'nt rich ;

And the valiant South would n't fight us

Till they died in the last ditch.

That Grant never won a battle,

And McLellan did n't know how ;

Nor John Brown to make Virginny skedaddle,

Before seventeen men and a cow.

That there never wan't no Homer,

Shakspeare wrote nary play;

That Byron's verse is dawdlin',

And must yield to Thackeray.

That Tupper's not в poet,

John Milton not sublime,

And Pope wrote his famous "Essay"

In execrable rhyme.

That Quintus Curtius never

Jumped into a hole,

Cornelia had no jewels,

Mark Antony no soul.

That there wan't no chaste Lucretia

For Brutus to defend,

And that *his brother* never

    Of Cæsar made an end.

That there is nary a devil,

    And Fisk was not a saint ;

That the "Wandering Jew" aint livin',

    And Bismark's course's a feint.

Now in all these things, from childhood,

    I've believed in as my breath,

And to have them rudely shattered

    Is worse to me than death.

And there's Darwin now that tells us,

    Our great grandfather was an ape,

And they can't disprove him no how

    By dissection, sermons, or tape.

Now you see I've always been proud of

My great genealogical tree,

And to find the root's so shaky

Is a very sore grief to me.

But three things yet I have faith in:

The Lovely, the Good, and True,

So I'll e'en take refuge, dear cousin,

In myself, "The Bay Fight," and you.

BEFORE the eternal throne of God
Grim Death in silence bent;
His fleshless hand had dropt the dart,
Its strength for once was spent.

A voice that none might disobey
Recalled his absent thought:
"A gem is wanting for the crown,
Which with my blood I bought.

Haste thee to earth, — from jewels rare
Select the brightest one

To shine within my diadem
　　Resplendent as the sun."

Death seized his dart and hurried on,
　　The world was reached too soon;
He paused before a brilliant hall,
　　For in that rich saloon

There sat a maiden young and fair,
　　Hope radiant in her eye;
Upon her cheek the blush of love,
　　Her heart in ecstasy,

For near her was the chosen one
　　Close nestled by her side;
A few short moons, and he might claim
　　His own, his promised bride.

Beauty and wealth and friends were hers,—

   Why should the spoiler come?

Why desolate that happy home?

   Why call her to the tomb?

Death paused! perchancè his callous heart

   A ray of pity moved:

He fain would spare that beauteous one,

   So fondly, truly loved.

He durst not, for the gem was found,

   The circle was complete;

Another perfect, peerless one

   He feared he might not meet.

His icy fingers touched her cheek,

   Blanched were the roses there;

J

Upon her lips he set his seal, —
Gone was the perfume rare.

Parents and friends and lover stood,
And watched the glazing eye;
Their forms convulsed, — their voices hushed
In speechless agony,

Until the mother clasped her hands
And called upon her God:
"Why am I doomed to suffer thus?
Why lay on me thy rod?

Why take from me my darling child,
So young and fresh and pure,
And leave the weary upon earth
Who life can scarce endure?

To many worn and wretched souls
   So little has been given,
That sweet to them would be the change
   From earthly woe to heaven."

Peace, mother! for the Saviour needs
   Thy precious one above ;
Thy jewel glitters in his crown
   Bought with his priceless love.

Free from the world's polluting touch,
   Untarnished it will shine ;
O trust thy treasure in His care, —
   ' Tis safer than in thine.

We have the will, but not the power
   To guard our cherished store ;

For Satan lies in ambush near,
　　And sin is at the door.

The road is broad, and many snares
　　Our footsteps lead astray ;
And if we tread the narrow path,
　　We stumble on the way.

We cannot keep ourselves from harm, —
　　Our treasures share our fate ;
Then let us bless Immanuel,
　　Who opes the heavenly gate,

And wears our jewels in his crown,
　　For none are missing there ;
No robber steals, nor moth, nor rust
　　Their beauty can impair.

And at the last great day may we

    Among them find a place,

And worthy deemed by God, to shine

    Around the throne of grace.

    *J

DEATH OF THE HEIR.

FRAIL as a fading flower,
   E'en from thy very birth,
I feared when first I saw thee, babe,
   Thou wert not long for earth.

But in that princely palace
   Methought Death would not dare,
To watch the jeweled cradle bright,
   And claim the infant heir.

Could not the robe of ermine,
   The costly, rich array,

The laces, gems, and roses, scare
  The spoiler from his prey?

No; vain was all this splendor,
  And vain the mother's sigh;
The idol must be broken now,—
  Her darling, he must die.

One earnest prayer to heaven,
  One long, loud cry of pain,
As if a heart were breaking too,
  And all is still again.

Death paused,—the eye grew brighter,—
  He did not send his dart;
That fearful cry of agony
  Had pierced his callous heart.

He passed to yon lone garret,—
   Nor fire, nor food, were there,
A babe lay on its mother's lap,
   Her hands were clasped in prayer.

"O God, have mercy on me,
   In pity take my child;
My brain is maddened fearfully,
   I am lonely, wretched, wild.

I have no food to give him,
   And Nature's fount is dry;
I cannot see him suffer long,
   But I can see him die."

Death stood a moment near her,
   Then raised his fleshless hand,

But ere it fell his arm was stayed,—-
  Stayed, and by God's command.

"Why didst thou leave the palace?
  Thy mission was not here.
Hast thou forgot my mandate stern?
  Hast thou no cause to fear?

Leave me this friendless woman,
  'Tis here that I abide,
And tho' she deems me far away,
  Am ever by her side.

She listened to a traitor,
  Was ruined and betrayed;
And deeply, darkly, fell the curse
  On her devoted head.

All who dare to break my laws
The penalty must pay,
But I will listen to her moans,
And wipe her tears away.

Her mournful wail hath reached me,
Her sins are all forgiven;
A mother's love is wafted, pure
As incense, unto heaven.

See this child, his cheek is pale,
But sure his form is fair,
And clustered round his lovely head,
Are ringlets rich and rare.

On his brow I've set my seal,
God's seal of genius bright,

And soon his large dark eye will glow
  With inspiration's light.

He is my own, my chosen,
  I've marked him from his birth,
And tho' his form is clothed in rags,
  He is of priceless worth.

No riches will I give him,
  But beauty, talent, health,
And from deep mines his soul will gain
  Imperishable wealth.

The great and gifted must not die
  In early infancy;
Never, until they have fulfilled
  Their glorious destiny.

To prove that even now in man
 God's image is not lost,
Tho' oft defaced, and scarce perceived,
 By sin and Satan tossed.

But in my chosen, bright it shines,
 Safe from all arrows hurled,
And like a beacon in the path,
 Illumes a fallen world.

Go!"   Death vanished from the scene,
 To question who may dare,
Why the poor outcast hath been spared,
 And why he claimed the heir.

CHARLIE.

AN angel dropped a ray of light
   To cheer us on our way,—
Gladly we hailed the vision bright,
   But soon it sped away.

A gem was ours,—we prized it well,
   And wore it with such care,
Valued it more than tongue can tell,
   When lost were in despair.

Our darling boy,—the gem, the ray,
   For us to love was given,
But deemed too pure on earth to stay,
   Transported back to heaven.

MARRIAGE IN A PRISON.

'TWAS not within the dazzling hall,
  Amid a throng of friends most dear,
And smiling relatives around,
  The heart of the young bride to cheer.

'T was not within the sacred aisle,
  Before the altar of our God,
With parents and with sisters near,
  The bridegroom and the fair one stood.

Where? dost thou ask!—Where, then, were they
  United in Love's holiest tie?

118

Where sealed that rite to mortal given

  By Him, the Ruler up on high?

'Twas in a dungeon dark and drear,

  With naught to dissipate its gloom,

With nothing genial to efface

  The horrors of that living tomb!

The man of God in silence stood,

  His eyes were raised as if in prayer,

And by his side two forms, as still

  As death, — they were the bridal pair!

One was a youth of noble mien,

  Ill-fitted for so vile a place,

And on his brow a loftiness

  That prison-walls could not efface.

His hands were clasped, his lips compressed, —
    He wore the calmness of despair ;
He looked as though his doom was sealed, —
    That he had outlived hope and fear,

Excepting when he glanced at her,
    That fair young being by his side,
Then agonizing was his gaze, —
    It seemed as if his spirit died.

And she was pale, but beautiful
    As when, in those bright hours of yore,
He revelled in her many charms,
    And Hope her smile of pleasure wore.

A solemn stillness reigned throughout,
    You might have heard each beating heart,

'Till broken by the preacher's voice:

  "Wilt thou love her 'till death do part?"

It seemed a strange, unearthly sound

  To him to whom it was addressed;

His eye was fixed, and oh! upon

  What dreadful object did it rest!

A scaffold near the casement stood!—

  'Twas there, oh God! that he might see

That, although innocent of crime,

  A sufferer he was doomed to be.

He answered not, nor bowed assent,

  But pressed that fair girl to his breast,

As when in days of happiness

  She knew it as her place of rest.

    *K

The blessing the then priest pronounced,

    And left them, for a last farewell

They wished to take alone, unseen

    By any in that gloomy cell!

Oh, what can woman's love efface?—

    Not dungeon, scaffold, chains, nor death;

She clings but with a firmer hold,—

    She loves until her latest breath.

She loved him when he was esteemed

    And honored by his fellow men;

And now her soul still turns to him,—

    Though all forsake, she'll not condemn!

BILL BUNTIN.

" YES, Warden, tell you I'm guilty,
  For there's no use in shammin' now;
I struck the man with a hatchet
  Along here, — right over the brow.

But I didn't mean to kill him,
  And I'm glad that he didn't die;
An' the gal, — we never tetched her,
  'An' if she says so, 'tis a lie.

Now, you see, my pal he wanted
  For to do the hull thing up brown,

To choke the gal an' to take her
    With us away out of the town.

But I'm consid'rable soft now
    On the wimmin, coz how you see
I thinks on one called Sary Ann
    Who tuk a great likin' to me.

So I said, ' No, let us leave her,
    And try our best to get away
And jine the ship, lest they cotch us
    If we long in the country stay.'

And then that little she-devil
    Began yellin' just like she's mad,
And so the perlice they 'nabbed us,
    And that was too thunderin' bad.

I got a chap to defend me

    Who said that he could get me clear,

But (twixt us) think he succeeded

    Far better in gettin' me here.

He told me that an *"a-lie-by"*

    Would be the fust thing he must prove;

And faith, he told enuff on 'em

    The hull heavens and airth to move.

He got a feller to swear, sir,

    On the book, straight up hill and down,

That he was a walkin' with me

    That night in a far Western town.

A place he'd never been into,

    Nor heerd of, not since he was born,

And so knowed no more about it
  Than a darkey a-grindin' corn.

And when they began to bother
  And asked what train he tuk that night,
He riggled wus than Aunt Sue's eels
  When the skin is cleaned off 'em quite.

And the tother one cross questioned
  'Till he was almost off his feet,
And looked 'bout as flat and sheepish
  As a young monkey just been beat.

Then my lawyer made a flourish,
  And said, 'Look where my client stands!
Did ye ever see a finer face?
  Think you blood can imbrue those hands?

O gentlemen, I remember
  When he was an innocent child,
And his mother a sweet creature
  With her dark eyes so soft and mild.

They lived in a pleasant cottage
  O'ergrown with 'some kind of stuff,'
With roses and lilies bloomin',
  And this world was heaven enuff.

And the mother would take her boy
  By the side of his snowy bed,
And invoke the Heavenly Father
  To shower blessings on his head.

Then the husband he would enter,
  And show the money he had made,

And tell how hard he had striven
   To grow rich in an honest trade.'

A pretty pictur, but bless you,
   A lie from beginning to end.
We lived in a rick'ty ten'ment,
   And don't believe God was our friend.

Mother was allus a yellin',
   And we slept on a dirty bunk,
And all the black eyes I seed'n her
   Father 'gin her when he was drunk.

But sometimes he wud be pleasant
   And hand me a penny or two;
But she never gave me nothin'
   But a taste of her leather shoe.

Now the judge he was a cute un,

    And he knowed well this was all bosh,

And often looked as he wanted

    To tell the flat feller to hush.

But he said 'the eloquent counsel

    Has now spoken and at full length,

But the fault of his arg'ment is

    It has more of beauty than strength.

Then he up and charged the jury

    In such a bold, common sense way,

That they brought the verdict 'Guilty,'

    After a mighty short delay.

And then the old judge he laid me

    Under a heavy prison ban,

L

But reckon p'raps I desarved it
    Just as much as another man.

But if Sary Ann should murder,
    And I knowed I could get her clear
By tellin' such a pack o' lies,
    There's a somethin' wud stop me here.

Darn me! I find it easier
    Far, for to strike a man a blow,
Than when my answer should be 'Yes,'
    To just 'straight forred' tell him 'No.'

I like you, Warden, you are frank,
    Know how to treat men on the square,
And feel that you will do by me
    What you think to be right and fair.

And there's one favor I wud ask,

    If ever Sary Ann should come

And wish to see Bill Buntin here,

    Please to say he is not at home.

That never in your hotel books

    Has he once registered his name,

For how should she know 'Thirty-two'

    Stands for Bill Buntin all the same?

But when my boardin' time is up,

    And I no longer need your care,

I'll find a room with key inside,

    And she that room with me shall share.

On Sundays I would like to have

    'The New Testament' in my cell,

I hate to hear the chaplin preach
  Sendin' all the bad folks to hell.

May be we'll get there fast enuff,
  Don't want him to give us a lift,
And if I die I'll take my chance
  To go along without his shrift.

And now good night, — I'll go to bed
  And try hard to get some sleep,
So I can dream of Sary Ann,
  And there's a vow I've made I'll keep."

A BURLESQUE.

GREEN and damp is the church on the heath,
Greener and damper the people beneath;

The long grass is twisted in knots so fine

That Œdipus' foot might ne'er untwine.

The slimy pond's fed by a vanished stream,

And over it sadly the moonbeams gleam:

A dismal swamp, as if Medean car

Had foundered there in days afar;

And Proserpine's hand might well disdain

To cull from it the golden grain.

The satyrs romped in wildest glee,

And there were seen the "Fatal Three."

Pegasus here might safely ride,

And the Arcadian stag be tied.

But hark! a scream and a whistle,

What fearful sound rushes through the thistle,

A snorting and tearing,

Bellowing and bearing,

As if all Cretan bulls were let loose?

And what is the monster

With its eyes shining,

Its head of brass, and coat of mail,

Feet of dragon,

And fiery tail,

The megatherium and ichthyosaurus combined?

A creature made of a fearful kind,

Like to the one by prophet seen

Before on earth it had ever been;

Prophetic of the day of doom,
Pushing its millions to the tomb.

Sudden a shriek! and what is there?
Jove's lightning, thunder, and despair!
Infants frying, strong men dying,
Mothers crying, sparks a-flying,
Splinters crashing, water splashing,
Maiden's dashing, iron clashing,
Horses prancing, conductors dancing,
Red lights glancing, surgeons lancing,
Brakemen screaming, colors gleaming,
Blood a-streaming, vapor steaming,
Ropes a-flinging, wounded bringing.
There never was heard such an infernal din
Since the gates of Hell were opened by Sin
To let Satan out and mortals in:

And the bones that were ground to bread
Might have fed the insolvent dead.

There stood upon a bank
A woman lean and lank,
Her long hair loosened from its hold
Like Medusa's snakes in slimy fold.
Can it be that her hand
In Christian land,
That suckling mite securely bound
With hemp, and fastened to the ground?
Ay! for in woman's darkest hour
No tract was brought with cheering power,
So she made for the track of shining steel,
That she might with her burden darkly kneel.
Like Antigone's her sacrifice:

A black face now is peering round

With inky cloak trailing to the ground,

Sudden a start, — a fearful yell!

Like a "South Sea bubble" the waters swell.

The Tritons make merry with Undine there,

And the mermaids comb their long locks in despair.

CRITICISM.

NOW isn't it provoking,
  When one tries to write his best,
To have the critics tell him
  That it will not stand the test?

That pentameters are wanting,
  And hexameters won't do,
No iambus in the metre,
  And the syllables too few?

That the trochees are at variance,
  And the verses will not scan,
And I don't know how to do it
  Except, it may be, a *man*.

138

That the metaphors are jumbled,

   The hyperboles obscure,

The verbs no antecedents,

   The rhetoric not pure.

And so they prune and clip it,

   'Till it's like a shaven lawn,

All nicely smooth and level,

   But every flower gone.

And thus they haul it over,

   And say "It is faultless now,"

And so is milk and water,

   But *blamed* tasteless, too, I vow.

You wonder what's the matter,

   Why it has lost its *vim;*

But think, as it is perfect,
  That it must be all your whim.

And when folks come to read it,
  They quietly lay it down;
You see not on their faces
  Either a smile or a frown.

And if to Holmes you should take it
  And ask why it was so flat,
He'd tell you as West, the artist,
  It decidedly wanted "That."

"That" means the fire of genius,
  The power to make men feel,
The very thing, when in the rough,
  That the critics from you steal.

I think it best, in writing,

   If we have a thing to say,

To let the words come bubbling

   Forth, in their own odd bright way.

Say something to make men laugh,

   Or something to make them cry;

And if there's a hitch in the metre,

   You can right it by and by.

We cannot write like Milton

   If we have not *got* his head;

Our Satan would be sappy,

   And our tree of knowledge dead.

But we may state an idea

   In language clever and strong,

M

Fit for a parson's sermon,

    Or a boy to *holler along*.

For a line well outspoken,

    Which a simple truth contains,

A volume of mere verse outweighs,

    For we hear the ring of *brains*.

And like the perfume of a flower,

    The rare sweetness of a tone,

The magic touch on canvas felt,

    All the beauty is its own.

Fresh from the Deity it came,

    We trace its heavenly birth,

And as a dew-drop will not

    Cease to purify the earth.

THE RAILROAD KING.

IT is fine to be an emperor,
  Or lord of a fleet to range,
It is great to be head of an army,
  But grand to be "King on Change."

It is plucky, when one is able,
  To get 'twixt the lion's jaws,
But pluckier far to "bully bears,"
  And then pull out their claws.

To fight the savage creatures up,
  And pull the fierce bulls down ; —

O ! I had rather do it
   Than wear Victoria's crown.

It shows what skill and foresight
   And industry can do,
Combined with an unerring aim,
   And perseverance too.

The world looks on with wonder
   To see the mighty thing,
And Young America's proud
   Of her great " Railroad King."

We have one bright example
   The feeble to sustain,
And only one, that daring
   May not presume in vain.

KINGS OF ENGLAND.*

TEN sixty-six brought conquering Willy,

Ten eighty-seven his Rufus Billy,

(In. whose reign first Peter the Hermit

Preached the Crusades without a permit.)

His brother Hal, who loved his ease,

In eleven hundred king we see ;

But eating once too many eels,

In ·thirty-five he ceased to be.

Then from France came Stephen Blois,

Who held the throne till fifty-four ;

* Written from memory of a similar piece read many years ago in an old newspaper.

From fifty-four till eighty-nine,

Great Second Hal, the crown was thine;

Then Richard First, named Cœur de Lion,

Till ninety-nine the throne we see on;

And John, ere twelve-sixteen, did sell

The crown that did not suit him well.

From twelve-sixteen till seventy-two

To Harry Third the crown was given,

When Edward Long-shanks, the king,

Began and reigned till thirteen-seven.

For twenty years Ned Second ruled;

The Third for fifty held the sway;

From seventy-seven till ninety-nine

The Second "Dickey" had his day.

Then comes the Red Rose from the North,

Who ruled till thirteen, Harry Fourth.

The Fifth for nine years held the throne,

The Sixth Hal died in sixty-one.

York's snowy Rose, Fourth Ned was tombed,

In eighty-three, the Fifth scarce bloomed,

When Richard Third, the monster grim,

Snapped off the rosebud's tender stem.

But Harry Seven, in eighty-five,

Proyed for poor Richard quite too tricky,

For in the fight on Bosworth Field

He sadly mangled England's Dickey.

In fifteen-nine came Sturdy Harry,

And six gay wives soon asked to marry;

From forty-seven Sixth Edward's life

Was six short years without one wife.

Red Mary next, who loved the groans

Of those who shriek on Romish pyres,

The first who ruled in petticoats,

The last that stifled human throats

With blood extinguished fires.

Alas! for the sad day when she

Began her reign in fifty-three.

In fifty-eight rose bright Queen Bess

In all her starry loveliness,

And shone in fair virginity

Until she set in sixteen-three.

Then James the First did Scotland give

Who held the throne till twenty-five,

When his son Charles began so fine,

But lost his head in forty-nine,

And Mr. Cromwell, by sheer stealth,

Governed the people a Commonwealth,

Till Charles the Second, merry king,

From sixty till eighty-five

Held fast the reins of government,

And kept the people all alive.

The Second James, an addle pate,

Fell from the throne in eighty-eight;

And Orange Will, in two-seventeen,

Made way for Ann, twelve years a queen.

For thirteen years reigned Georgius One,

(Though the Pretender sought the throne;)

Till seventeen-sixty George the Second,

When George the Third mounted the throne on
    which he sate

For sixty long, long years of state.

In eighteen-twenty George the Fourth began a
    ten years' reign.

Fourth William reignéd seven years,

Then turned to dust again;

In thirty-seven Victoria

Took up the sceptre where it fell.

O may she reign without a war

And govern all her subjects well.

"NEITHER DO I CONDEMN THEE: GO AND SIN NO MORE."

WEARY and worn the Saviour went,
　Upon a noted day,
Unto a sacred mount where oft
　Retired he to pray.

What means that bustling, anxious crowd?
　Whom do they bring along?
Taunted by bitter jibes and jeers,
　By obscene word and song.

A wretched woman, gazing round,
　In agonized surprise,

But not one look of sympathy
From all those cruel eyes.

And yet her form would speak her one
Nurtured in happy home.
What force compels her, in this guise,
The city streets to roam?

Is there not one of all she loved
To stay their fierce desire?
Why are her fortune, fame, and dress,
Like trailing in the mire?

The Tyrian scarf so rudely torn,
She may have worn a bride,
And on her now bare bleeding feet
The jewelled sandals tied.

A costly veil perchance was thrown
  Over her lovely head
To hide her beauty, and her ear
  By love notes sweetly fed.

And as they near the place where sits
  He, their rejected king,
Their voices in brutal tones
  Through heaven's high arches ring.

This woman whom we bring to thee
  Is stained by foulest sin,
Her shameless act proclaims her all
  Corrupt, without, within.

Moses commanded in the law
  That all such outcasts be
  N

Stoned even unto very death ;
But, Master, what say ye ?

Then Jesus paused a man to find,
Who God's law had not broke,
A lesson I will teach them now,
And thus he calmly spoke,

" If there is one among you all
Of pure and blameless life,
True to his God, himself, and friend,
As well as to his wife,

Let him take up the largest stone
Within this rocky bed,
And hurl it with what force he may,
At her defenceless head."

Then quietly he turned away,

  And wrote upon the ground ;

When next he raised his eyes, not one

  Of all those men he found,

Only the woman standing there,

  Preferring that a stone

Should crush her senseless to the earth,

  Than Christ to meet alone.

Gently he moves him to her side,

  Takes her resistless hand,

Raises to his her streaming eyes,

  And says in accents bland,

"To cast the first stone at thee, found

  'Mong thine accusers none ?"

In accents mournful she replied,
  " My Lord, not even one."

And prostrate, grovelled at his feet
  As he addressed her then,
"God's mercy may extend to all,
  Neither do I condemn.

I pardon thee, but not thy sin,
  For that thou must atone,
Thy sullied purity be cleansed,
  Not by a blow of stone.

Before me is outspread thy life,
  And all the anguished past :
The struggle, and the lure by which
  The tempter won at last.

I know thy weakness and his strength,

    For I have felt his power,

And might, but for my Father's aid,

    Have yielded in that hour.

Should he once more with glozing tongue

    Thy spirit dare assail,

If on me heavily you lean,

    I tell thee he must fail.

But if he then the victor be,

    Sure barred is Heaven's door,

Obey my first and last command,

    'Go thou and sin no more.'"

    *N

SATAN'S ADVICE.

OLD Satan one day was quite ill at ease;
Very hard his Majesty was to please,

For he had wandered full many an hour,

Vainly seeking one whom he might devour;

At last he chanced on a simpering dame,

All unknown to him except by her fame,

And he chuckled and said: "I've found a soul

Over whom I can have supreme control;"

And snugly then he ensconced himself there,

Just as she arose from her knees in prayer.

Her dear father died on that very day,

And folks whispered—but what, I will not say;

But this I do know: from that very hour

The Devil o'er her had the fullest power.

First of all, he espied a shrinking girl,

Fragile and modest and pure as pearl,

The loved ward of him who now was no more,

Whom the leech's craft was vain to restore,

Who was wont to call her his joy and pride,

None dearer to him in the world beside;

Whose hand, cold in death, was powerless now

To wipe the sad tears from her fair young brow,

Or shield her from one who, with fiendish art,

Was trying all means to break her young heart.

Soon as Satan saw her, so pale and still,

He said to his friend: 'Now, dear, for the Will,—

Be led by me, and I will clutch for you

What the law will allow, and far more too.

Yourself shall inherit, all shall be thine;

Your dear father's will, what is it to *mine?*

You hate that young girl, you hate all the name;

Your feelings and mine are about the same.

They serve me in part, but you are my own,

Both body and soul, flesh, sinew, and bone.

We can fool some people — they will not dream'

That you can be other than what you seem;

When we have robbed the ward of her just due,

We will smile and pray, and build houses new.

The sacred cup we will place to our lip,

And drink damnation at every sip;

And as we pass down the broad solemn aisle

We will stop and chat, bow, simper, and smile.

A few, perhaps, will start back with affright,

For, seeing through pure and heavenly light,

My snaky form they may chance to descry

Hidden deep in the cell of thy dark eye,

Or gracefully coiled in thy jaunty cap

The knowing may find me taking a nap;

On thy lips may revel in thoughtless glee,

'Till some one exclaims: 'I know that is *he!*'

Then down in thy soul I will quickly hide,

And caress my children, Envy and Pride;

And you must be bland as a summer sea,

And say; 'Madam, my love, do call on me!

And the dear little ones — hope they are well?'

While within I am raging, black as hell.

As for your kin, you must say to them, 'Come,'

For in your palace you know there is room,

And the world would censure if they should starve;

They have not the wit their fortunes to carve,

So you must provide them all with a place,
But do it with such a niggardly grace
That, worn and vexed, they will venture to say
They 'had rather live on a penny a day.'

But it is time we disposed of your ward;
Can it be you fear the anger of God?
You tremble, for you remember the blow
When his red right hand laid your loved ones low.
I plot and plan, but His will is complete;
When he strikes I lie crouching at his feet;
Though I have oft defied, disowned His power,
I never could yet for a single hour
Shield the wretch when summoned before his throne
To answer for sins in the body done;
But if you are willing to serve me true,
I will do the best that I can for you.

Of this world's goods you shall have your full share,

The ward you can leave in my gentle care ;

I will show you how to be rid of her

In a quiet manner, without a stir. ·

You cannot beat or burn or starve or drown,

Such things would be published throughout the town ;

But there are weapons to crush out her life

More deadly far than the assassin's knife:

You can trample on all that is pure and good ;

You can crush the bright spark of womanhood ;

You can dry the tear, you can freeze the soul ;

You can get her so under your control

That she dare not speak or move at her ease

For fear that her tyrant she might displease.

You can teach her distrust ; to play a part:

To scorn all emotion, feeling, and heart ;

You need not address her one kindly word,

And when her young soul within her is stirred

By charity, love, friendship, or pain,

Laugh, and tell her she has nothing to gain.

The world is too wise for such follies now,

And Mammon the shrine at which we all bow.

And when your disdain, hate, coolness, and scorn

Have made her wish that she never was born,

And driven her forth from her guardian's door,

Never, never, to cross its portals more,

You can say to all who may chance to come:

'I miss my dear friend since she left her home.'

I know your dead father with solemn air,

This poor child confided unto your care,

To love and cherish, to counsel and guide,

'Till death should place you once more by his side,

But what do we care for his wishes now?

We have all his money, the world must bow;

Whate'er it thinks we will keep it at bay,

The cock he must crow, the dog have its day."

Until the day when the Father of all

Who have ever lived on this earthly ball

Calls each to account for talents misused,

For all blessings slighted, scorned, or abused;

When each soul must appear naked and true,

To meet the Great Eye that pierces us through;

When, stripped of splendor that dazzles below,

We stand before God as his friend or foe—

Say, how will you meet him? with scorn and pride,

Defying him there as here you defied?

When he asks for his own, give him the cloth

Where the talent's wrapped of so little worth?

O

Or vainly on rocks and mountains will call
To shield you from Him, Avenger of all?
Too late for mercy, your doom will be scaled;
No light in your soul will e'er be revealed;
Satan will claim you, as here he has done;
Hell's gates will be opened, both will be one.
But still the ward in a forgiving tone
Wrestled thus for her soul before the throne.
God knows I hope this doom will not be thine,
Though deeply you have injured me and mine;
But we are taught by Him, in his blest creed,
To forgive all sins both by word and deed,
And truly I trust that the pardoning power
Bestowed on the thief in that last sad hour
May extend to thee; and blood from that side
Wash thy scarlet sins white in its crimson tide;

That those eyes that have never yet shed tears

Except for thyself, thy own griefs and fears,

May be raised to Jesus for hope and rest,

And, thy vile soul purged, find peace on his breast!

TRINITY.

O GOD, the Father, give me strength
  To keep thy perfect law,
Never to swerve from duty's path
  Or from the right withdraw.

O God, the Son, our pattern pure,
  Teach me unselfish love,
To value still my neighbor's good
  All other aims above.

O God, the Spirit, send me grace
  To bear each coming ill,

168

To bow in meekness 'neath the rod,

Nor murmur at thy will.

Power, Love, and Grace, "The Triune God,"

Thyself to me impart,

That one I may become with thee,

In mind, in soul, in heart.

*O

DARKNESS AND LIGHT.

ONE moonlight eve I had been musing long
Upon the fitness of the universe;

On Heaven and Hell, the seen and the unseen,

The immutable and the mutable;

Why wrong should be instead of the great right,

What use in pain of any kind or sort,

Whether to rack the body or the mind.

A Supreme Being must be supremely wise,

And all an emanation from his will.

Can He be, then, part evil and part good?

Or is the former in man's thought alone?

No; the body's anguish is an evil

Which sanity can ne'er pronounce a good.

Then, if the All-Wise does permit it here,

Will it not cling to us in other worlds,

There to torment with perhaps greater power?

And for the lost is there a place prepared?

Lost,—and how lost? In God's broad universe

Is there a molecule or an atom lost,

Annihilated? when each thought we breathe,

Each word we speak, had an existence,

And must have one still, part of the great whole.

If matter's not created, is spirit?

Perchance each but change their form, and spirit

Is only a subtler kind of matter

That each particle with life possesses,

Tho' it eludes the chemist's fine analysis.

We have the power of changing matter:

This essence God retains in his own grasp, —
To us the secret confided never.

And so I mused 'till I began to doubt
God, Heaven, the world, my own identity.
All was black chaos as before the words,
"Let there be light," and so I wandered forth,
And met one upon whom men looked with dread.
His life was thought unholy to have been,
Though what his crime was, none vouchsafed to tell.
The future, it was said, he might unveil,
But through his evil master; therefore few
Dare question him. The poor folk crossed themselves
If he approached, and gave him "right of way."
Seldom he spoke, and no interest took
In aught that e'er another did concern;
Sufficient seemed he to himself alone.

I simply bowed, and thus accosted him :

It is said that from some dark source you gain

Knowledge beyond our ken. To me impart

The secret of eternal life or death.

Tell me, if in far brighter orbs we live,

Or sink to deeper night without a hope ?

Are we immortal as we've ever been ?

Or does the soul commingle with the dust ?

O, great magician, if you have the power,

Impart the truth and give my soul relief !

A ray of moonlight fell upon his brow,

And as he raised his beaming eyes to mine

He seemed inspired by spirit not his own.

He answered not, but from his well-worn coat

A book he took, and placed it in my hand ;

Open it fell, and on a page I saw

Written, " Read this, and you will be wiser."

I hastened home my treasure to explore,

And, knitting, there sat my aunt Agatha,

An antique spinster, all gaunt, grim, and gray;

Her skin, hair, dress, of the same neutral hue.

Her life was one great duty,— pleasure none;

Each day rolled on in chill monotony;

Yet she accepted it and murmured not.

Had she a staff on which I could not lean?

Her all, summed up, was but to mind the house,

The thriftless poor to feed, and children teach;

Herself seemed ever absent from her thought,

Except as wanted for another's good.

(But even she her romance: In a box,

Securely locked, there was a faded flower,

A bit of ribbon, a worn, wrinkled glove,

Yellow with age, and tiny crumpled notes

Whose perfume seemed to speak of wasted love,

So subtle in its nature even now.)

Youth, wealth, and beauty were my happy fate ;

Courted, admired, loved, without a foe,

And many friends, or those that I deemed such,

Who rode, drank, smoked with me as I desired.

And women, too, hung breathless on my smile,

For I had learned the witching art to make

The softer sex yield captive to my will.

And yet with all I envied Agatha.

The book I opened, and began to read.

Can it be ! And is it, then, the Bible

The sage has given, wherein to find the truth ?

The Bible which, from boyhood, I have learnt,

'Till each line is familiar to my ear?

I glanced upon the leaf, and every word

Seemed to be fraught with meaning new and strange,

As tho' the light from a far distant star,

For ages wandering through unbounded space,

Had just reached earth and fallen on the page;

So clearly now did each great truth appear:

And, inspiration guiding, I read on.

By searching deep thou ne'er canst find out God,

Nor wonders vast that from thee He has hid;

But still thy duty is the no less plain.

Waste not thy time in vain imaginings,

Which do thyself, as well as others, wrong;

Thou hast a field of action in the world,

Thy talents there use for thy fellows' good;

Shake off the slime of slothful egotism,

Give of thy knowledge to the famished crowd,

Share with thy brother all of hoarded wealth,

Leave not a soul if thou canst do him good;

Let thy loud voice as a clear trumpet sound

In bold defence of innocence when wronged;

From truth weed error, the oppressed one cheer,

And make the world the better for your life.

Do it, not only you may save your soul,

But for the earnest love of Christ's great work.

There is no merit in any act of thine:

A draught of water to a starving beast

Is, in God's eye, a deed of charity,

As thousands lavished on a pauper's home.

And why? Because each, like water dripping,

Tends to dissolve the granite selfishness

Deeply imbedded in the human heart;

P

That sin of sins perchance the only one;

Let us review God's moral law, and see.

Idolatry, profanity, and work

For other or ourselves upon his day,

Disregard of every natural tie,

Fraud, lying, lust, murder, and coveting,—

Can they not all be traced to one great cause?

And deeply Jesus probed the human heart

When he demanded of the *good* young man,

Whom culture fine had kept from grosser sin,

"Give to the needy all thy cherished store,

And follow me unto the bitter end."

That test his selfishness could not endure,

And well the master knew the fearful fact.

Food to the starving beggar,

Clothes to the destitute child,

Warmth to the freezing widow,

A draught to the sick man wild ;

Rest to the woman weary,

A light to the captive's cell,

And Christ hath promised truly

That with us it shall be well.

THE CLOCK OF THE PASSION.

6 o'clock.

WITHIN a chamber, at the Feast,
The Lord from Heaven above,

Washes his poor disciples' feet

In meekness and in love.

7 o'clock.

The bread he breaks, the wine he pours,

"Christians, where'er you be,

Eat of my body, drink my blood

In memory of me.

180

There's one among you who hath oft

Sworn to be ever true,

Who, this night, will betray his Lord,

And shew what man can do."

8 *o'clock*.

From Cedron to Gethsemane

Behold him passing now,

His followers are only three

Who faithful keep their vow.

9 *o'clock*.

"O, Father, may this bitter cup

Pass from thy much loved Son;

Let me not drink it to the dregs,

But yet thy will be done."
*P

And to his weary followers now,

"Could ye not watch one hour?

Watch and pray often, if ye would

Vanquish the Tempter's power."

10 *o'clock.*

Again that agonizing prayer,

An angel comes to cheer;

His bloody sweat rolls on the ground,

His darkest hour is near.

11 *o'clock.*

He goes, alas, to meet his doom;

His foes he cannot miss;

The once loved Judas on his lips

Imprints the traitor kiss.

12 *o'clock.*

> They bind him with those cruel cords,
>
> Taunt him with brutal jest,
>
> And lead him to Jerusalem
>
> To torture there with zest.

FRIDAY, A. M.

1 *o'clock.*

> Before the High Priest, Caiaphas,
>
> Falsely accused he stands;
>
> Witnesses swear his life away,
>
> His blood be on their hands.

2 *o'clock.*

> Thrice Peter doth deny his Lord,
>
> And thrice the cock doth crow,
>
> All now forsake the Lamb of God,
>
> No aid from man below.

Jesus on Peter turns his eyes

With look of tender love,

The bitterness of that reproof,

All censure far above.

3 *o'clock.*

Over those holy, precious eyes

Th' accursèd cloth is bound;

They smite, and in derision ask,

Whose hand inflicts the wound?

4 *o'clock.*

When Pilate questions, "Are you king?

Are these your subjects here?"

"I have a kingdom," he replies,

"Where title deeds are clear."

5 o'clock.

> Herod in puerile mockery,
>
>> Clothes him in garments white,
>
> Altho' well fitted to the Lord
>
>> Of Innocence and Light.

FRIDAY, A. M.

6 o'clock.

> The people loudly clamor for
>
>> Barahbas's release,
>
> Knowing that Pilate's only fear
>
>> Is to disturb their peace.

7 o'clock.

> The knotted scourge cuts long and deep,
>
>> Blood follows from each stroke,
>
> No heart to share his agony,
>
>> None where compassion woke.

8 *o'clock.*

> A crown of thorns is on his head,
>
> A reed put in his hand,
>
> A purple robe upon him placed
>
> By the derisive band.

9 *o'clock,*

> In many ways doth Pilate try
>
> For his release a plan,
>
> But failing all, brings Jesus forth
>
> And says, "Behold the man."

10 *o'clock.*

> Still he protests in him no fault
>
> For which he ought to die,
>
> But yields at last to the loud call
>
> Of Priests, to crucify.

11 *o'clock.*

> His cross he bears, and murmurs not
>
> Beneath his heavy load,
>
> 'Till Calvary's red mount is reached,
>
> Where now must die a God.

12 *o'clock.*

> Nailed to the tree, behold him now
>
> Fastened between two thieves;
>
> What agony upon that brow, —
>
> How his strong bosom heaves!

FRIDAY,   P. M.

1 *o'clock.*

> His love and mercy not forgot,
>
> Unto the thief is given

The promise he shall share to-day
With him the joys of Heaven.

And for his enemies he prays,
"They know not what they do.
Father forgive them for my sake,
This deadly wrong to you."

2 o'clock.

· The scorching agony of thirst,
A moment fills his mind,
But he rejects the proffered gall,
Again his thought is kind:

Love for a mother wakes his heart,
Care for her days to come,

And of his loved disciple asks

That he will take her home.

3 *o'clock.*

The fearful tragedy is o'er,

"'Tis finished," so he cries,

" Father, my soul is in thy hands,"

And bowing, meekly dies.

4 *o'clock.*

With their bright, cruel lances keen,

The soldiers pierce his side,

And from it blood and water flows

In a pale crimson tide.

Q

5 *o'clock.*

From the vile cross the Saviour's borne

By friends, unto his tomb,

And an appalling darkness fills

The universe with gloom.

THE REMAINING PIECES WERE WRITTEN BY

RELATIVES OF THE AUTHOR OF THOSE

PRECEDING THEM.

TO MY DAUGHTER ISABELLA, ON HER TWENTY-FIRST BIRTHDAY.*

YOU request me, dear Bell, to pen a simple lay,

To celebrate th' event, your twenty-first birthday ;

But, my dear child, know you that genius I have none,

That the Muses were absent the time I was born.

How can I presume, then, to call upon their aid,

For what Nature cruelly denied when she made ?

Truly they would deride my attempts at " sublime,"—

Bid me presume not the mount " Parnassus" to climb.

---

* Written by Mrs. Charlotte P. De Wolf, and revised by her loving daughter, who wished to preserve the piece for the friends of the family.

"Step from your sphere, you have neither talent nor
    wit;

Go home to your duties and think well how to *knit*."

Think, did you say? and can the Nine solve me a
    thought?

A problem whose solution has never been wrought?

That mysterious "ignis fatuus" of the mind,

Outshoots the lightning's speed, and leaves meteors
    behind;

An unwearied tyrant that never quits the brain,

And ever the centre of pleasure, or of pain;

Without which, man were a leaden mass of matter,

Devoid of all conception of a hereafter.

Can there be mind where no thought ever finds a
    place?

Only the brute can answer,— not the human race.

But methinks you observe this is no fitting lay

To be written to me upon my natal day.

It is true, my dear child, my words have not expressed

The deep-seated feeling ensconced within my breast;

My heart's poetical, my thoughts rudely sublime,

But niggard Ideality denies me a rhyme.

But e'en now I will commence with a dog-trot verse,

And a few reminiscences try to rehearse.

Can it be, dear Bell, you are indeed twenty-one?

Time has flown since the hour you were *not born a son.*

"A score of girls," the gossips said, "we'd hoped a boy,"

"For a girl, after all, can be only a toy."

But it mattered naught unto her who gave you birth,

For she was the very happiest thing on earth;

And whether God's great gift was a girl or a boy,

Her heart and soul were filled with ineffable joy;

Heaven showered choice blessings upon your infant
  head, .
The softest eider-down composed your tiny bed,
Your slips were woven by India's finest loom,
Rich lace adorned that brow as yet unknown to gloom;
And thou wert beautiful, with eyes of azure blue,
And a rare expression, as if the soul shone through.
Carnation cheek, rosebud mouth, teeth as white as
  milk, .
And skin like Orient pearl, its texture soft as silk:
A Hebe in beauty, and Hygeia in health;
Truly a fortune in self of unbounded wealth.

Your infancy was cradled in a princely home,
A regal mansion where fine taste and beauty shone;
Corinthian columns supported the stately pile,
So imposing that strangers stood gazing awhile;

All admired this spacious and lofty dome,

And none that entered its precincts e'er wished to roam.

The splendid saloons were hung with China's crimson
 silks,

And golden eagles spread their wings to guard their
 jewelled beaks;

The floors were clad in "Brussels," and ottomans had
 place,

With Egyptian mantels polished so that one might
 see their face;

The chandeliers of crystal were from Venetia's store.

And scattered round were volumes of Byron, Scott,
 and Moore,

There were alabaster graces by Canova well designed,

And sweet harmonious music to elevate the mind,

And there assembled oft, were beauty, wit, and grace,

And costly mirrors to reflect each bright and happy face,

And did you wish for perfume your senses to regale,

The conservatory. open, its sweets you inhale.

There sat the goddess Flora, in majesty of state,

Clasping her exotics, from mountain, sea, and lake,

All wishing to be the one presiding genius,

And the choice fell on,— whom? the night-blooming

 cereus.

The cardinal myrtle called him "parvenu;"

Said they had rather be classed with rude feather-few,

That his birth-place was in a thick jungle or bog,

That his life had been passed round an old rotten log,

That his perfume was sweet, but exhaled in the night,

That one must be bad to prefer darkness to light ;

There was the amaranth whose life is forever,

On whom Time makes no change, and Death cannot

 sever.

The "Passion Flower," glorious, meek, and sublime,

A fit emblem of Him whom man owns as divine;

And numberless roses, but none called "the elite,"

Save, "Heaven born Alexandrine," "Moss," and "Tea"
  sweet;

All these roses formed wreaths, that the cherubs
  entwined,

Beauty, virtue, and love, were the symbols designed;

The love of the nightingale for this sweet flower,

Is the theme of the poet for many an hour,

And the loving chaste orange tree blossomed there too,

To form wreaths for the bride ever spotless and new,

And the century-plant whose bloom denotes decay,

Warning us that earthly bliss will soon pass away;

There were singing birds from grove, forest, and
  mountain,

And goldfish that swam in a clear crystal fountain.

Each spring, in the garden, queen Flora held high
    state,

And invited her courtiers to a grand fete,

And on the verdant, smooth, sparkling, emerald lawn,

They danced and made merry, from evening till dawn,

First the coxcomb Narcissus, on his slender stalk,

Paid his devoirs so fine to tall Miss Hollyhock,

Then came the Dowager Peonia with a red face,

Sadly wanting in beauty, deficient in grace,

The haughty "Crown Imperial," proud of his name,

And of the pearl in its petals languidly came,

Next the Tulips, clad in rich robes of rainbow hue,

Flaunted their gay colors near the tall Southern yew,

And looked with contempt on the pure Snowdrop so
    white,

And the Violet too modest, shrinking from light,

The Hyacinth, Cowslip, and Syringa sweet,

Wooed the trembling Anemone from her retreat;

And, bowing low, came the Dandy, lion of fate,

Who can tell, without doubt, who is true to his mate;

Th' odoriferous Lilac, and blooming Snowball,

Then came dropping their petals through the bright
      gay hall,

The sweet Lily, stiff Primrose, and dainty Heartsease,

Were invited to dance, and as long as they please;

The "Prince's Feather" nodded low to Miss Goldcup,

And asked the honor with her lady-ship to sup;

All the Asters were there, and each branch might be
      told,

And 'twas whispered John Jacob would wed Mary
      Gold.

The Coxcomb came prinking, so afraid it was late,

But he hoped Miss Carnation would find him a mate;

R

Miss "Fleur de Lis" accepted with grace his white
  hand,

But that she was royal gave him to understand,

The Acacia wove his golden chain, link by link,

Around the lovely daughter of Carnation Pink,

The splendid Oleander flirts with Magnolia,

The fickle Hydrangea with grand Centipolia,

The gallant Sweet-William, known to be a rich heir,

Caused a blush on the Rose, when he whispered
  "You're fair."

The princely Dahlias flaunted in their regal pomp,

But doffed their lofty airs when ready for a romp;

The gallant Larkspur ogled proud Miss Touch-me-not,

And Miss Primrose muttered "He surely has forgot;

Now I should not countenance such a sad *roue;*

I wonder what the Bachelors near me would say?"

"Trailing Creeper" crawled along with his measured
    step,

And said he could dance, but should need a little help,

The Honeysuckle, Clematis, and Columbine,

With affection their tendrils o'er all do entwine;

Then there was the Belle shining superbly at night,

But whom a ray from Aurora will change to a fright.

Next comes the bold, brazen-faced flower of the Sun,

Who unveiled, her God follows throughout his long run.

The Wall-flower stood apart, th' Abbey his retreat,

His blood-stained robe told tales of murder and defeat.

"Johnny go to bed." spread his couch with Rose-mary,

And said he should leave, for sleepy he was very;

Next came drowsy Poppy, nodding, yawning along,

And declared it was time to disperse the gay throng,

That a drop from his petals would put them to sleep,

But he said there was danger in drinking too deep,

So they took his advice, and all left the gay scene,

And Aurora shed light on the emerald green.

When the harvest was gathered, and Summer was past,

Pomona, the queen, said "That the first should be last,

And Artemisia, Stockjelly, and Flora's bouquet,

Should come to her party ere passing away,

Also fragrant Mignonette, and blue-eyed Lucerne,

The rare beauties of which all that look may discern."

And the Sweet Pea came slowly winding down the stair,

To meet her friends in Phlox, who had assembled there.

And soon the ample, luxurious board was spread,

But the Daisy dared not rear her sweet modest head.

Cornucopœia presided with lavish hand,

And the wants of her guests seemed to well understand.

There were peaches so delicious, juicy, and large

A luxury unknown in Cleopatra's barge,

The pears of St. Michael, and Burdelue mellow,

Their tints of all hues, brown, crimson, green, and

    yellow ;

There were grapes, apricots, nectarines, fine and rare,

For on them had been bestowed the tenderest care ;

There were apples, too, intended for more than show,

And naught to me is sweeter than an apple blow.

When Memory retraces my childhood's golden hours,

She pauses to inhale the fragrance of those flowers ;

The Anana was Pomona's delight and pride, —

I preferred the "pyrus malus," close by its side ;

And grapes in rich festoons entwined the mossy seats,

Their tendrils trying to perform some fantastic feats.

O days, when no care preyed on that light heart of

    mine,

No blighted hopes to retard the eagle wing of time,

    *R

But a change came o'er Eden, no dream of the brain,

But a curse terrible as that of Eve to Cain;

The mad whirlpool engulphed my fairy bark of bliss,

Judge of the woe caused by calamity like this;

So I sigh o'er the past, and weep o'er the present,

And dread the future with its evils attendant.

I cannot, I will not, sit here supine and sad,

In this state of inaction shall surely go mad;

Time is thought to be well skilled in the healing art,

But knows no panacea for a breaking heart.

No thunder rolled, nor lighting flashed, to sound the
    dread alarm,

The natural world, as if to mock, put forth her every
    charm.

What cared she whose heart might break on that sad,
    bitter night,

The joyous morn was ushered in with all its pristine light,

No day returned to cheer my sad and sickly heart,

The aim was sure and Time fails to extract the dart.

Is there in trackless forest, where human foot ne'er trod,

An elixir for our woes known only unto God?

Nature doth abound with specifics for relief,—

Is there no healing balsam for a heart torn with grief?

As I entered the dark and dismal mine, with feelings
     of horror and dread,

I was met by a demon who turned my heart to balls
     of lead.

Then I hailed the gay lark as he soared high through
     the air,

And urged to be wafted to a region more fair;

"O tell me, as you carol from planet to star,

Is there no blest fountain to heal the heart's deep
     scar?"

"Oh, no," said the songster, "I have flown round this
    zone,

And found no cure for the soul that's bleeding and torn."

But there is, there must be, some far glorious orb,

Where our tears do not flow, and our hearts do not
    throb;

Where pure spirits dwell in celestial realms of light,

No chrysalis there, no long and wearisome night,

When shall I emerge from this vile aurelian coil,

And like the freed insect fly from all care and toil,

Safe to Heaven to recline on my Father's breast,

In the mansion of love, there forever to rest.

THE OLD MAN'S LAMENT.

TO THE CHILDREN, AND GRAND CHILDREN, OF MY MOST
EXCELLENT FRIEND, THE LATE HONORABLE WIL-
LIAM BRADFORD, OF BLESSED MEMORY.

A MERRY Christmas to you all,
  Says poor Nathaniel West;
Long may my patron's children live,
  With health and plenty blest.

Let's call to mind the happy days,
  (With pleasure sure we may,)
When your good father rul'd the Mount *
  With hospitable sway.

* Mount Hope, R. I.
209

Father of all beneath his roof,
  Where plenty always flowed,
His bounty he, with joyful heart,
  On every guest bestowed.

Where'er he met the coming guest,
  The beggar, or the Count,*
The language of his heart was still,
  You're welcome to the Mount.

Bright glowed the fires, round whirled the spit,
  The willing cellar bled;
The table groaned beneath its load,
  'Till every guest was fed.

Oft have I heard that table roar,
  While mirth and wine went round;

---

* The sobriquet of the late worthy and venerable Jonathan Russell.

The happy host, and joyous guest,
  Made all the hall resound.

The kitchen caught the joyful glee,
  And echoed back the strain,
While rallying round the second cut,
  The cider flowed amain.

O kitchen! scene of all my joys,
  Where want was never known,
Where squashes, hams, and runnet bags,
  In brilliant order shone.

Oft in the field this furrowed brow
  Has sweat beneath the fork;
But oftener in the kitchen sweat,
  While eating beef and pork.

Even now it makes my brow perspire,
  And sets my throat to itching,
To think of mugs of cider drank
  In that same glorious kitchen.

O halcyon days, O happy times,
  To memory most dear,
Thanksgiving then came every day,
  'Twas Christmas all the year.

Old Uncle Song, and Hannah Green,
  More lucky far than I,
While yet their master blessed the earth,
  In good old age did die.

But I have in his service lived
  Full three and twenty years,

And never of the morrow thought,—
   Devoid of cares and fears.

To tell of half his good to me,
   My tale would never end ;
God bless his soul—I'll say no more,
   I've lost a real good friend.

But now the times are sadly changed,
   I'm old and piteous poor;
In tatter'd rags, with feet unshod,
   I shiver at your door.

No good roast beef my waistcoat lines,
   No cider warms my heart,
No cotton shirt or woolen hose,
   To ward off winter's smart.
    S

Could your good father view me thus,

From realms of heavenly bliss,

In accents such as angels use,

His language would be this:

"Child, clothe the naked, house the poor,

And feed him at your board;

'Tis my request, 'tis God's command,

You'll here have your reward."

THE COUNTRY SCHOOL.

GOOD morning, girls, come take your places,

I'm glad to see you've all clean faces;

Jane, Grace, and Lucy, come and read,

If you for once can be agreed —

You quarrelled so last time you read

You almost mazed and crazed my head.

Well — now begin — "Lucy what's now,

A *desput* frown is on your brow?"

"Ma'am, Gracie says she's up a top,"

"So I be, ma'am," — "Hush! one at a time — stop.

You wan't here yesterday, Miss Grace,

So at the bottom take your place;

215

Now, Lucy, read"—"and Jesus said,

Hath not where to lay his head."

"You've skipped a line—what are you about?"

"Why, ma'am, the words are all thumbed out."

"Let Jane begin—what's now to pay?"

"Ma'am—Lucy snatched my book away."

"Give her the book—stop all such jests."

"The foxes have holes, the birds have nests."

"Why, how you read—go take your work

And hem this towel in a jerk,

Don't let a single stitch be seen!

Patty, you've kept this shirt quite clean.

Hannah, this copy isn't good,

You've wrote as long as Betsey Wood,

And see how she comes on. You, Jane Whiting,

And you, Grace Thompson, bring your writing.

This t's not crossed, this i's not dotted,

And goodness suz see how it's blotted."

"Ma'am, Bila Townley's eating apples,"

"I see her and shall rap her knuckles."

"I've used my yarn, ma'am." "Very well,

Now hear the younger children spell.

Silence them boys there,—George, leave knocking."

"Ma'am, Judy Bostwick's done her stocking."

"Ben Atkins, you're at the head, spell physic,"

"Ph—th"—"that spells phthisic."

"Them words are hard and we can't spell 'em,"

"They don't study, ma'am,"—"So I tell 'em.

Go learn your words." "Ma'am, Ben said vow,"

"I didn't, ma'am—she lies—so now,

She was afeard cos she said gizzard."

"Katy, what's that," "ampersand," "no, izzard"—

"What's that?" "Great O;" "That?" "Little topped I;"

"There's crooked S, great banging J,—

Go and sit down, you Hannah Hawkin,

Stand on the floor and tell whose talking,"

"Sam Jones playing pushpin with John Gray,

Grace Thompson talking with Polly Bray."

"Ma'am, I han't spoke a single word,"

"Jane Whiting talking with Nancy Bird;"

"This sum don't prove you must carry more,

Six and four are ten"—"I knowed that afore."

"Ma'am, Sally hunches me, I hain't no room"—

"William, you're late, school's almost done,"

"Well—mammy sent me on an errand

About our cow to Parson Truand,

And said if how you axed the reason,"

"Ask, not axe," "why I warn't in season,"

" Well, hush — you 've said enough upon it,

Let every girl get on her bonnet ;

Boys make your manners — Polly Broom

Be here in time to sweep the room."

www.ingramcontent.com/pod-product-compliance
Lightning Source LLC
Chambersburg PA
CBHW030126030726
47498CB00007B/2565